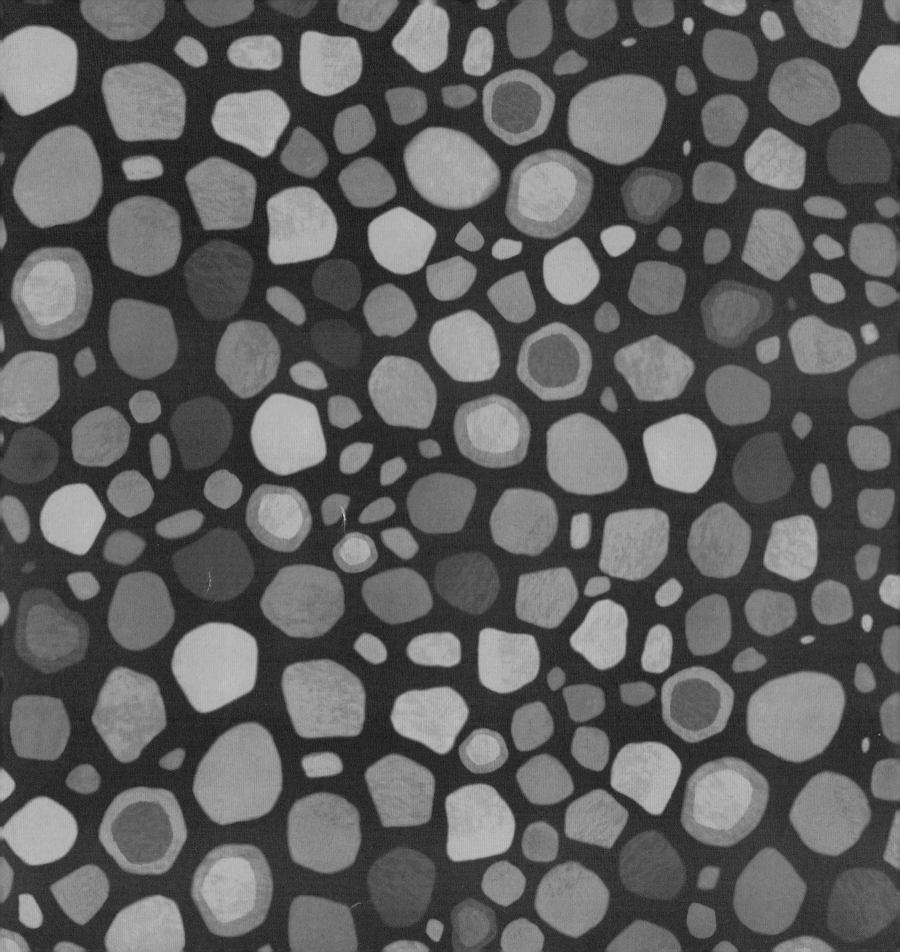

A TEMPLAR BOOK

This book is based on the episode *Mazu Takes a Chance*
from the TV series *Gigantosaurus*™.
Screenplay by Jacqueline Moody.
The TV series *Gigantosaurus*™ is created and produced by Cyber Group Studios.
Based on the original characters created by Jonny Duddle in the book *Gigantosaurus*,
first published by Templar Books in 2014.

First published in the UK in 2021 by Templar Books,
an imprint of Bonnier Books UK,
The Plaza, 535 King's Road, London, SW10 0SZ
Owned by Bonnier Books,
Sveavägen 56, Stockholm, Sweden
www.templarco.co.uk
www.bonnierbooks.co.uk

1 3 5 7 9 10 8 6 4 2

ISBN 978-1-78741-683-3

Adapted by Harriet Paul and Mandy Archer
Edited by Lydia Watson and Carly Blake
Designed by Kate Wakeham
Additional design by Adam Allori
Production by: Ché Creasey

Printed in China

GIGANTOSAURUS

THE LAST DRAGONFLY

templar
books

Mazu was on a mission to find a way into a secret grotto. There was just one thing standing in her way – a giant dinosaur-eating plant! In a split second, Mazu found herself hanging upside down by her tail.

"I really don't think that plant wants to be friends with you," called Tiny.

"I'LL save you!" Rocky cried heroically.

But Mazu didn't need saving. It was all part of her plan! The plant spat Mazu out, setting off a series of traps and clearing a path to the grotto's entrance.

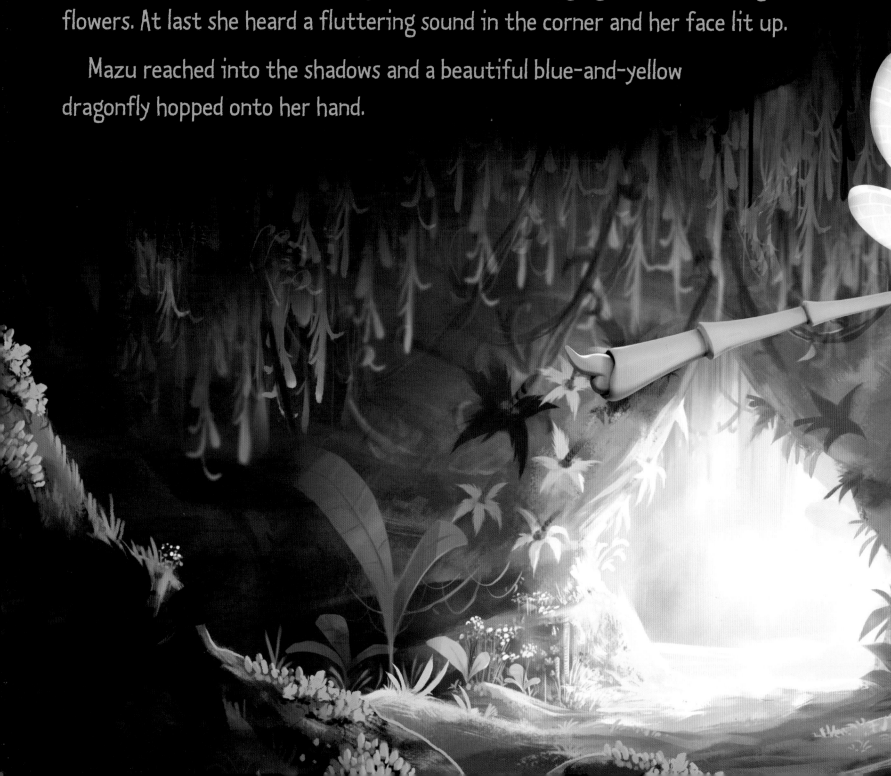

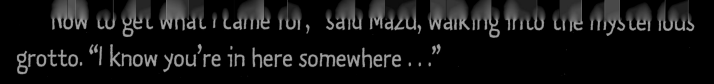

"Now to get what I came for," said Mazu, walking into the mysterious grotto. "I know you're in here somewhere . . ."

The little dino searched among the thick moss, hanging vines and strange flowers. At last she heard a fluttering sound in the corner and her face lit up.

Mazu reached into the shadows and a beautiful blue-and-yellow dragonfly hopped onto her hand.

Mazu's friends were waiting for her down by the river. When she came out of the grotto, they were very surprised to see that all she had found was a dragonfly.

They wandered along the riverbank with the little bug riding on Mazu's tail.
"You know Mazu. She'll do ANYTHING for science!" said Tiny.

"This dragonfly isn't just ANY bug," Mazu explained. "She's the last of her kind, and she's ready to have babies. If I don't find her a safe spot to lay her eggs, she'll go EXTINCT!"

Suddenly, two raptors, Totor and Cror, sped past and snatched the bug.

The two sneaky raptors had stolen the dragonfly and they weren't about to return her anytime soon!

"Give me back that DRAGONFLY!" Mazu yelled angrily. "She's very rare!"

But the raptors leapt out of reach and waved the insect in the air to tease the little dinosaurs.

Mazu thought fast. "If you give me back that dragonfly, I'll . . . erm . . . give you something even rarer – a SCALE from GIGANTO!"

"You'd have to be the bravest dino on the planet to do that," sneered Cror.

The raptors sniggered and turned back towards the jungle. "You get us the scale," Cror shouted over her shoulder, "and you can have the dragonfly back!"

The challenge was set. Now Mazu HAD to find Gigantosaurus!

While the others searched for Giganto, Bill found something he liked better – yummy yellow honey dripping from a dinobee nest.

"I don't think Giganto's up there," laughed Tiny as a drip landed in Bill's mouth. "That's just a bunch of bees."

As the friends walked on, they heard a strange humming noise behind them –
and it was getting closer. Uh-oh! Bill had disturbed the . . .

DINOBEES!

The friends sprinted through the jungle to get away from the swarm of bees.
They came to a sudden stop when they bumped into something big and green . . .
with VERY large teeth . . .

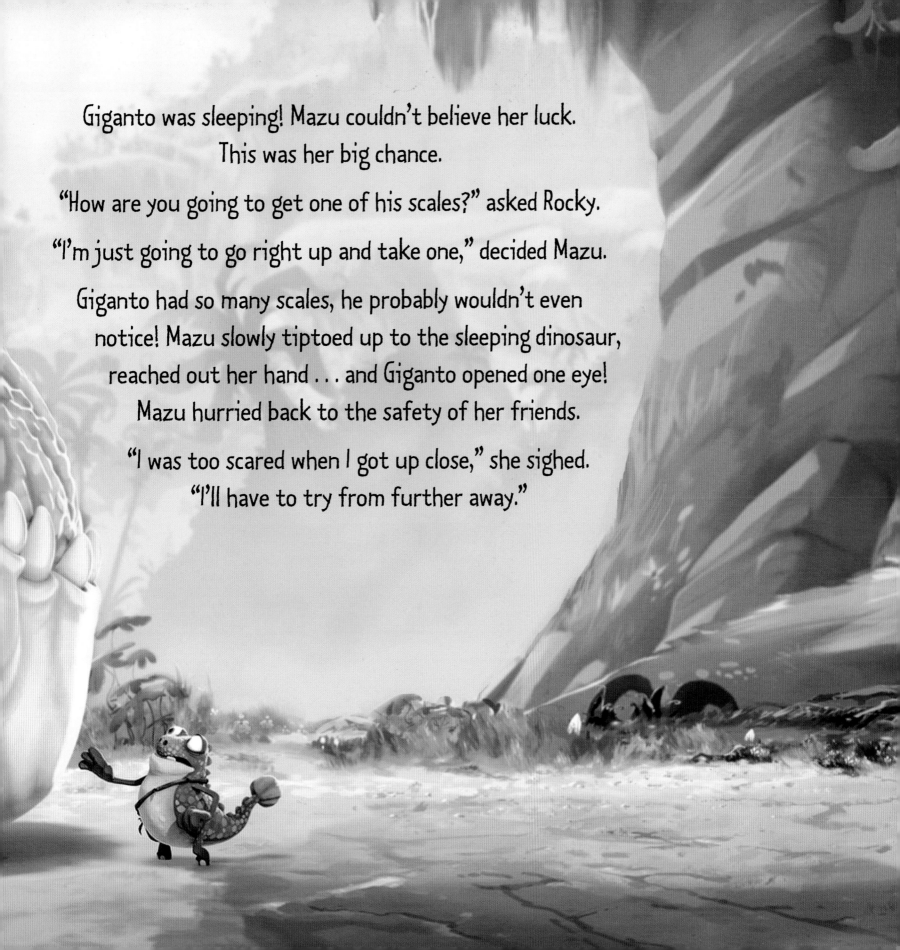

Giganto was sleeping! Mazu couldn't believe her luck.
This was her big chance.

"How are you going to get one of his scales?" asked Rocky.

"I'm just going to go right up and take one," decided Mazu.

Giganto had so many scales, he probably wouldn't even
notice! Mazu slowly tiptoed up to the sleeping dinosaur,
reached out her hand . . . and Giganto opened one eye!
Mazu hurried back to the safety of her friends.

"I was too scared when I got up close," she sighed.
"I'll have to try from further away."

Mazu thought quickly. How could she get hold of one of Giganto's scales from a distance? When she spotted a hanging vine and a sharp rock nearby, she had an idea.

"I'm going to swing this vine over Giganto," she explained, tying the rock to the end of the vine. "The rock will cut the scale right off his back!"

She swung the vine around her head and practised catching a flower.

But as she looked down at the sharp rock, Mazu realised something.
"Wait . . ." she said, worried. "What if Giganto can get hurt, just like us?"

Mazu needed to find another way to get a scale from Giganto.
She wasn't going to give up on her dragonfly friend.

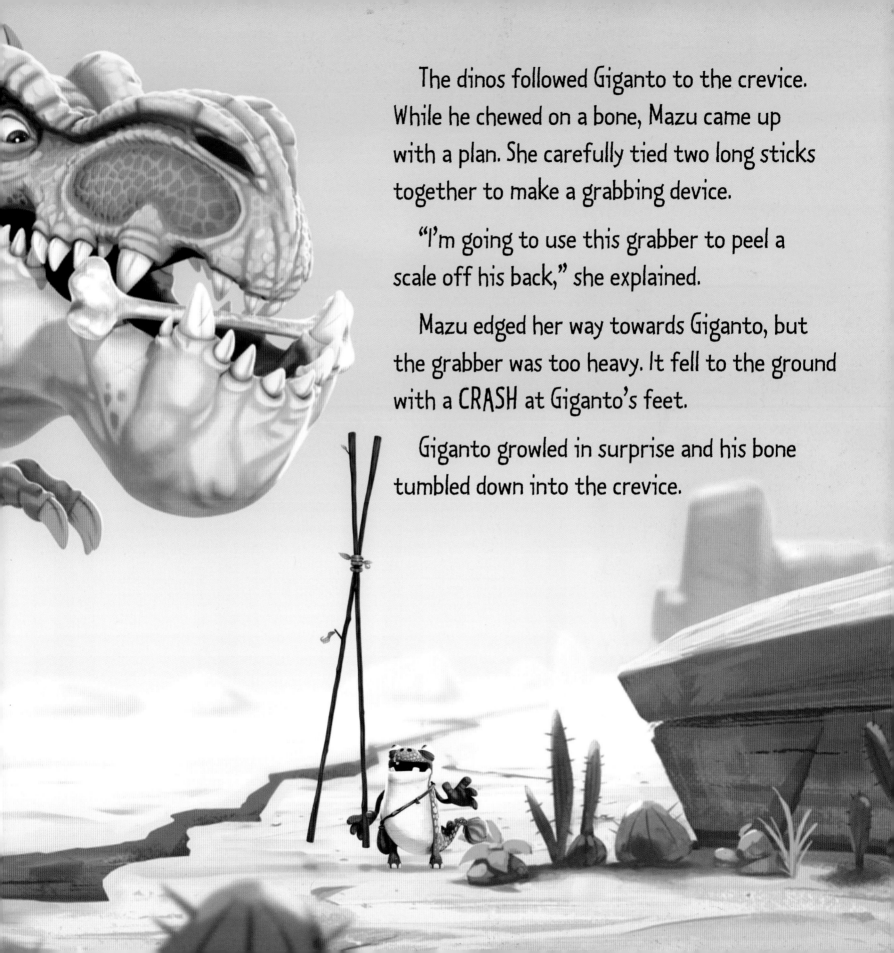

The dinos followed Giganto to the crevice. While he chewed on a bone, Mazu came up with a plan. She carefully tied two long sticks together to make a grabbing device.

"I'm going to use this grabber to peel a scale off his back," she explained.

Mazu edged her way towards Giganto, but the grabber was too heavy. It fell to the ground with a CRASH at Giganto's feet.

Giganto growled in surprise and his bone tumbled down into the crevice.

Gigantosaurus looked very cross. He had lost his lunch!

"Everything I've tried has failed," Mazu groaned in despair.

"Don't give up," urged Rocky. "You can fail loads of times and still succeed!"

Bill nodded. "That little dragonfly is counting on you."

Her friends were right! Feeling determined, Mazu picked up her grabber and ran back to the crevice. At least she might be able to save Giganto's lunch! Mazu carefully lifted the bone out and pushed it towards Giganto.

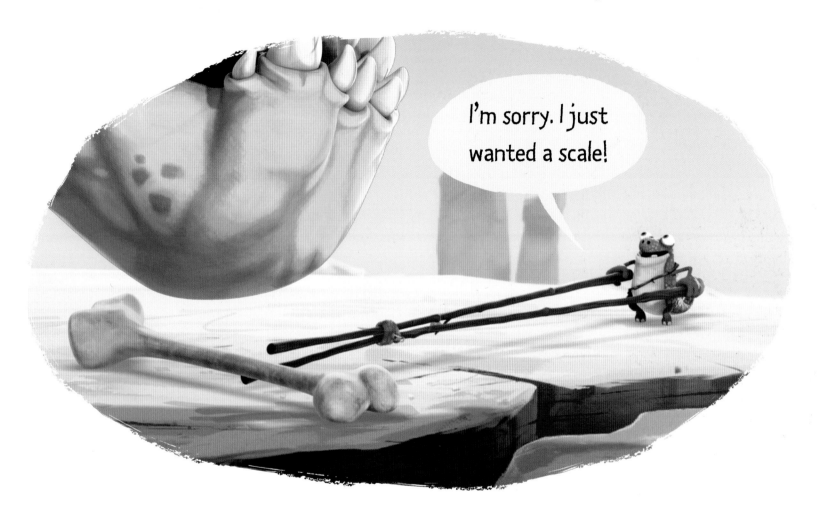

Giganto didn't look so cross anymore and he stomped away to eat in peace. But it still hadn't solved their other problem.

"I'll NEVER get the dragonfly back!" Mazu said sadly.

Mazu's friends weren't used to seeing her upset. She was such a brainy dino, they knew she'd think of a way. She just needed to use her head.

Back in the jungle, the raptors had left the dragonfly inside a small cage made of twigs and gone off to make more mischief.

Totor spotted a suspicious-looking vine stretched across the path.

"It's probably one of Mazu's crazy traps," he smirked.

The raptors jumped over the vine – and landed on a rock that tipped upwards . . .

"Uh-oh!" they yelled. Within seconds, the pair were tied up and dangling from a tree!

Mazu leapt out from her hiding place and rushed over to free the dragonfly. The little creature flew into the air, then settled happily on her rescuer's hand.

"You did it, Mazu!" cheered her friends. They knew she would find a way!

Your smart ideas saved the day!

Let's get you to a safe place to lay your eggs!

"I guess I didn't need Giganto's scale after all," said Mazu thoughtfully. "But imagine if I HAD managed to get one . . ."

Just then the ground began to shake. Giganto was back! He peered down at Mazu, then rubbed his back against a tree as if he was scratching an itch . . . and a single scale fell to the ground.

Thank you!

A little later, Mazu was lying on the bank of the river watching proudly as the dragonfly eggs hatched. Around Mazu's neck was a very special scale necklace.

A tiny baby dragonfly fluttered into the air. Soon there was another and another! Mazu skipped after them happily. She had tried her very best and now the dragonfly species was saved.

"Can I wear Giganto's scale now?" begged Bill. "PLEASE?"

"Sure you can," said Mazu.

"I'm GIGANTOSAURUS!" roared Bill, showing off. "I'm not scared of ANYTHING – ARGGH!" He squealed with fright as another of the little bugs buzzed by.

"Except for a baby dragonfly!" giggled Tiny.

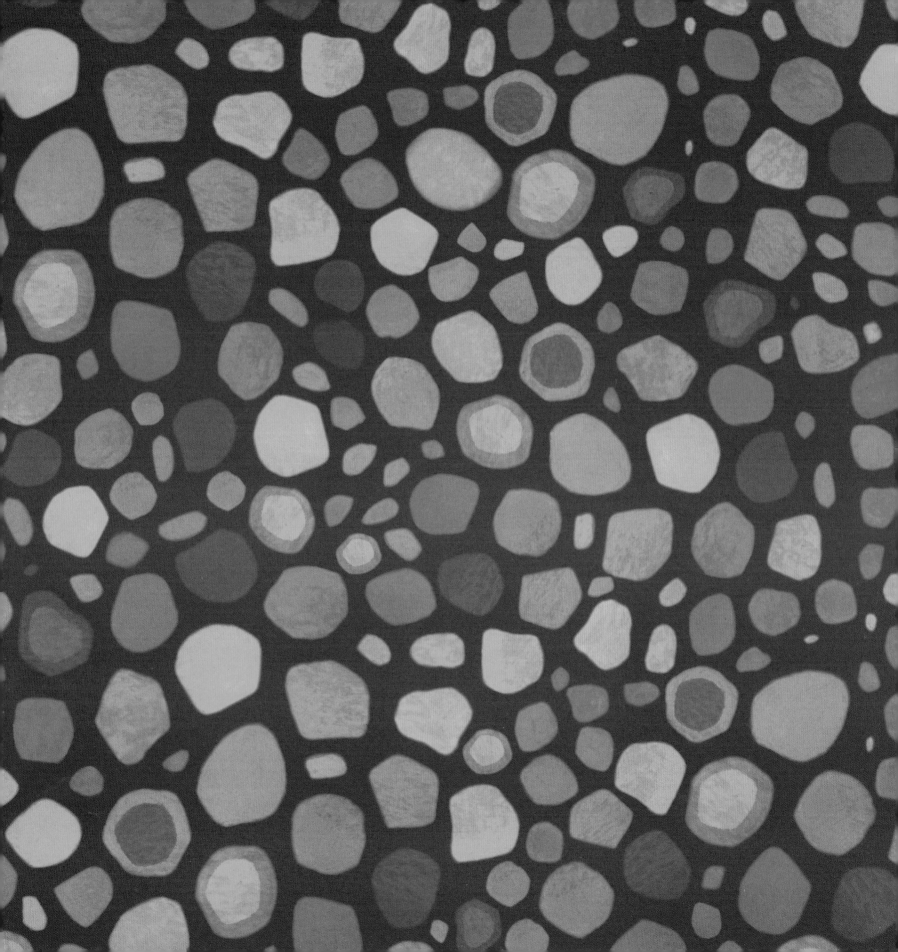

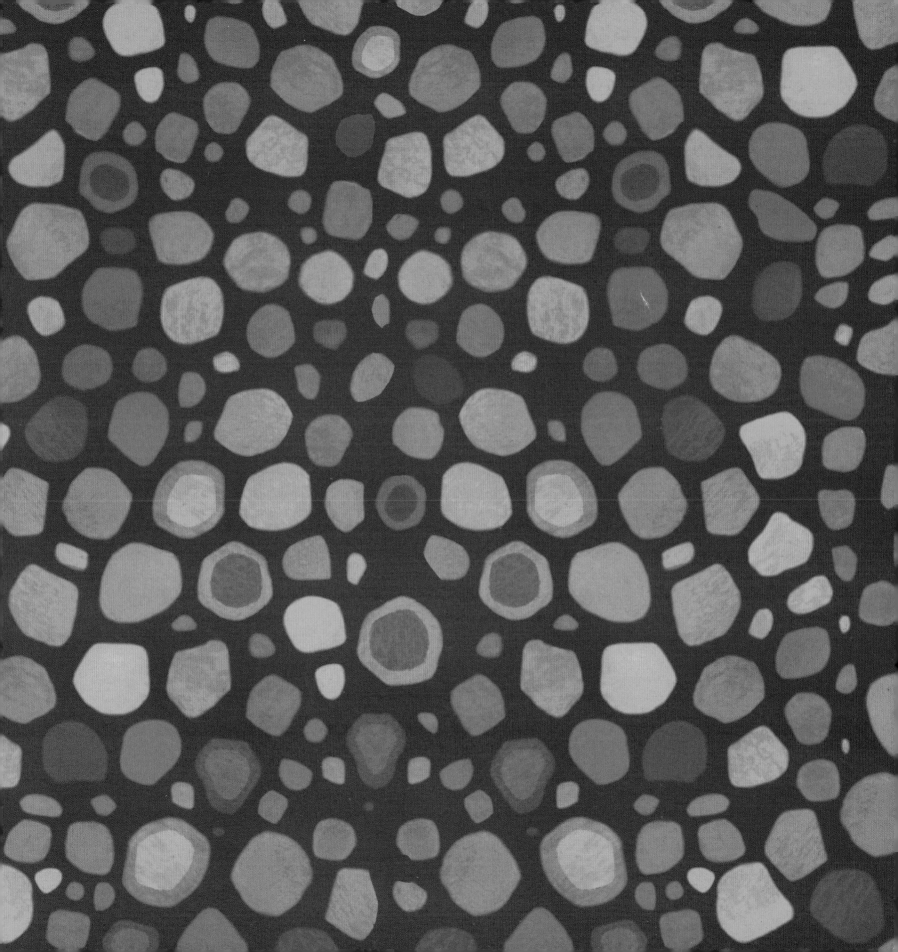

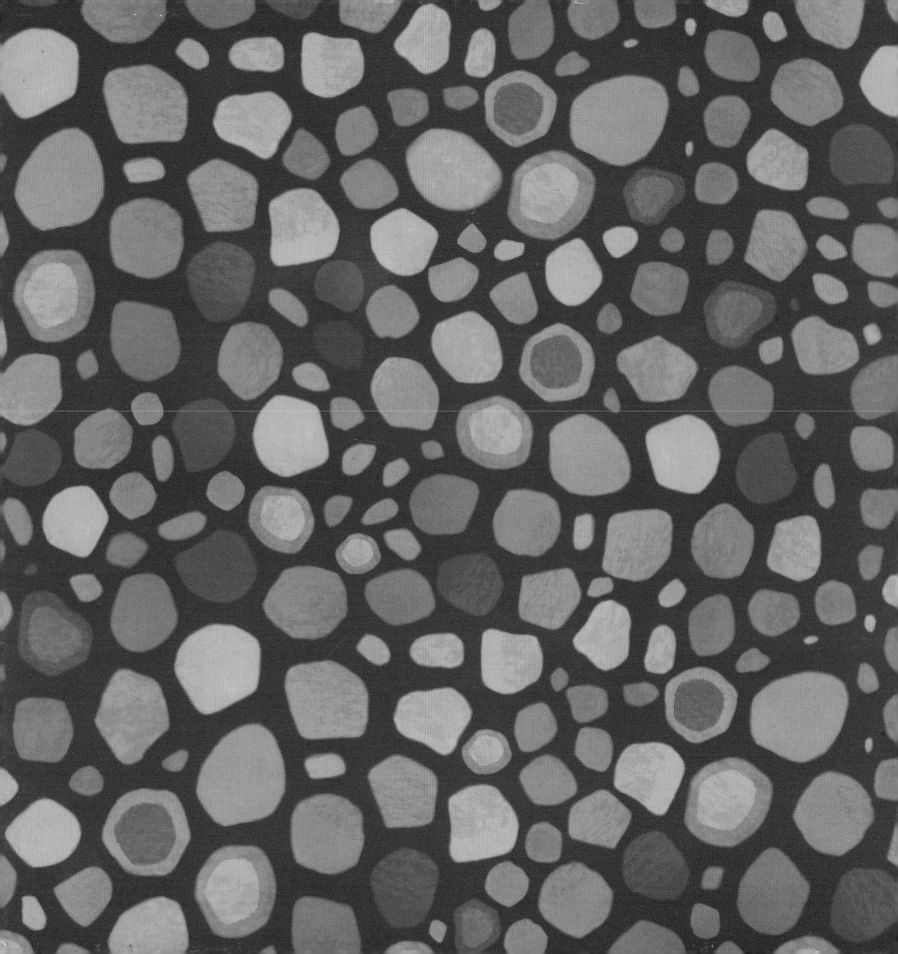